Farm Stories

Cover illustrated by Mary Morgan
Title page illustrated by Kathy Wilburn

Publications International, Ltd.

Conforms to the safety requirements of ASTM F963.

Fisher-Price trademarks are used under license from Fisher-Price, Inc.,
a subsidiary of Mattel, Inc., East Aurora, New York 14052, 1-800-432-5437.
Manufactured for and distributed by Publications International, Inc.

Text and illustrations © 2000 Publications International, Ltd.

Published by Louis Weber, C.E.O.
Publications International, Ltd.
7373 North Cicero Avenue
Lincolnwood, Illinois 60712

Manufactured in China.

8 7 6 5 4 3 2 1

ISBN: 0-7853-4187-0

Contents

Contents

Contents

Contents

Good Morning Farm

Illustrated by Lee Duggan
Written by Sarah Toast

Every morning Rooster happily greeted the sun with a big, "Cock-a-doodle-doo!" But this morning he was especially excited. Rooster scratched his claws on the ground. He could not wait to crow.

Rooster hopped up onto the fence, puffed out his chest, and spread his wings. Then he let out an even bigger and louder crow than usual.

"Cock-a-doodle-doo! Cock-a-doodle-doo!" he crowed. "Cock-a-doodle-doo-doo-doo!"

"My, my, that is a special greeting this morning," said the bright sun.

Rooster hopped up and down on the fence and said to the sun, "I have a surprise that I cannot wait to show the other animals!"

"Well, you had better go wake them up then," said the sun. Rooster agreed and flew off. He flew as fast as he could over to the pigpen.

When he got there, Rooster found Pig sleeping.

"Wake up!" said Rooster. "I have a big surprise! Come with me and see!"

"I am surprised you woke me up," Pig said with a startled oink. "But I will come with you and see this big surprise of yours, just as soon as I am ready."

Pig slowly yawned and stretched. Then he rolled in the mud, not once, but twice. Pig was ready now.

Rooster and Pig hurried over to the barn. There they found Cow sleeping in her bed of straw.

Rooster gently landed on top of Cow's head. "Good morning, Rooster. Good morning, Pig," mooed Cow.

"I have a big surprise to show you," said Rooster.

"How exciting! I cannot wait to see it," said Cow as she shook off some straw. "Let's get moving!"

Rooster, Pig, and Cow went out to the pasture to look for Lamb. They finally found her sleeping by some flowers.

"Cock-a-doodle-doo-doo-doo! I have a big surprise this morning," said Rooster.

"Rooster, this must be a good surprise. You seem very excited," said Lamb as she wiped her eyes. "I wonder what it could be."

"Cow and I would like to know too," said Pig. "Why don't we all go together and see!"

"Come with me!" said Rooster.

Rooster flew up into the sky ahead of his friends to lead the way. Pig, Cow, and Lamb followed.

"Where are we going?" asked Lamb.

"Are we almost there?" asked Pig. "I am hungry."

"Me too," said Cow.

"You will just have to wait," said Rooster.

As they walked on, Pig, Cow, and Lamb tried to guess what the big surprise could be. What special thing were they about to see?

"Maybe it is a new trough," oinked Pig.

Pig had a wonderful picture in his head. He saw himself eating out of a huge trough filled with delicious food.

There would be lots of corn and bread and tasty apples, which were his favorites.

 "Maybe it is a new pasture," Cow said. She saw herself eating in a huge field of sweet clover. Then she saw herself taking a nice nap on the soft grass. Lamb thought that Cow and Pig had some good guesses. But she did not think Rooster would be excited about a new trough or pasture.

"I cannot guess what it could be," Lamb said.

Pig, Cow, and Lamb followed Rooster all the way to the other side of the farm. They finally stopped when Rooster perched on the wooden fence outside of the henhouse.

Rooster turned to the other animals. "You are probably wondering why I called you all here," he said as he puffed out his chest.

"Yes, we are," oinked Pig.

"Tell us more," mooed Cow.

"Well, look over there," crowed Rooster. He walked across the yard to the henhouse. The animals heard a strange sound. It was a peeping sound.

What could it be? Then the animals looked over by the hay and saw what made those noisy sounds.

There were six newly hatched baby chicks! They were taking their first breaths and waving their little wings. They looked up at Mama Hen and Rooster, and then they chirped. Rooster was a proud papa!

"What a great surprise!" said Pig, Cow, and Lamb. They all listened to the chicks cheep and chirp. One chick even said a cock-a-doodle-doo, just like papa.

Old MacDonald Had a Farm

Sweetly Sings the Donkey

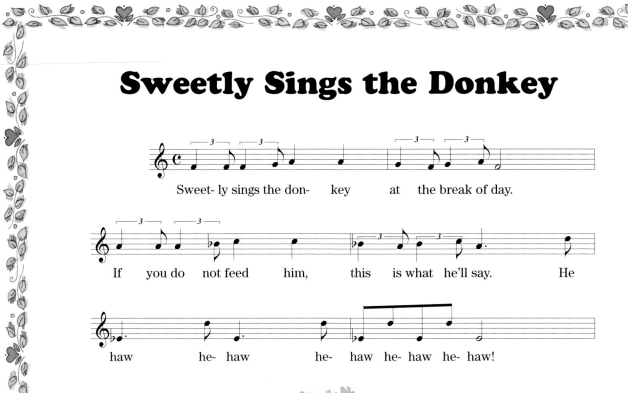

Sweet- ly sings the don- key at the break of day.

If you do not feed him, this is what he'll say. He

haw he- haw he- haw he- haw he- haw!

Farm Donkey

Illustrated by Robert Masheris
Written by Catherine McCafferty
and Lisa Harkrader

This is going to be a busy year for Dinky! She is three years old now, so she can help with the chores around the farm.

Dinky is learning to wear a light saddle, a halter, and a bit. She is learning to walk on a lead rope with the farmer at her side.

When Dinky is not learning, she is busy playing. She plays with the farmer's children. Dinky trots around the barnyard with them. Then she grabs the farmer's hat and runs off with it.

Dinky likes it when the farmer chases her. The farmer likes it, too. They run out the gate and down the road. The farmer laughs when he finally catches her. There will always be time for play, but now Dinky must help the farmer work.

Farm Donkey

Farm Donkey

The farmer and his family raise flowers that they sell at their roadside stand. Each morning the farmer loads freshly cut flowers into the baskets that Dinky carries on her back. Dinky thinks the flowers smell as fresh and sweet as newly cut hay. She does not mind carrying the flowers, but the farmer minds when Dinky tastes them!

One morning, after a late night rain, Dinky stops on the way to the stand. The farmer calls to her, but Dinky does not move.

The road on the way to the stand is very muddy today. Dinky's small hooves sink into the mud. She pulls hard to pick up her front hoof. She pulls so hard that she slides in the slippery mud. Dinky does not like slipping and sliding. When the farmer sees the problem he leads Dinky over onto the grass.

When Dinky and the farmer come back from the roadside stand, Dinky helps the farmer plow his fields. The plow is heavier than the flower baskets, but Dinky is very strong. She takes her time and works hard.

Dinky's little feet do not trample the soil as much as a horse's big hooves do. And Dinky can work harder and longer in the hot spring sun than a larger horse can.

Dinky is smaller than most horses, but her ears are a lot bigger than a horse's ears! The farmer always knows when Dinky is paying attention to him by watching her ears. Dinky turns her long ears in the direction of the farmer's voice so she can listen to him. And Dinky is a lot steadier and more patient than a horse.

Farm Donkey

Farm Donkey

Dinky's patience and steadiness are important once summer comes. The farmer sells strawberries now. But instead of carrying them out to the stand, he lets families come and pick the strawberries that he grows in his fields. The families bring baskets and buckets and fill them to the top with the farmer's plump, red berries.

Many children come with their parents to pick strawberries. The children like to visit Dinky. They pet her and talk to her and scratch her between her ears. Dinky enjoys all the attention.

Sometimes Dinky gives the children rides around the barnyard. She does not mind. The children are not as heavy as the farmer's plow, and they give her big hugs after their rides. Dinky really misses the children when they leave.

In the fall the children come to see Dinky again. The farmer sells pumpkins now, and the field is full of children picking out their special Halloween pumpkins. Dinky gives hayrides to the children, and she helps haul really big pumpkins out to the road for the farmer to display.

One cool night, as Dinky looks out from her shed, she sees something creeping toward the farm. It is the same size as the farmer's dog, and its fur is reddish orange, just like the farmer's pumpkins.

Dinky knows this animal is not welcome on the farm. As it moves across the pumpkin patch toward the barn, Dinky sounds an alarm to call the farmer. "EE AW! EE AW!" she brays over and over again. The farmer runs out to see what's wrong just as a fox hurries away from the farmyard.

Farm Donkey

Farm Donkey

As winter approaches, Dinky helps the farmer get ready for the cold weather. She helps bring in the hay. The hay is important for all of the farm animals in the winter.

For Dinky, the hay will serve as food and bedding. Dinky likes to sleep lying down, so a bed of hay is just right for her. The cows and the chickens like to sleep in the hay, too.

Once the hay is stored, Dinky goes with the farmer into the woods to gather firewood. The firewood will help keep the farmer and his family warm during the cold winter. Dinky likes to take these walks. She is very sure-footed on the uneven ground.

When the farmer finds a fallen tree he cuts it into pieces. He piles the pieces onto a sturdy sleigh, and Dinky pulls it back to the woodshed.

One frosty morning the farmer takes Dinky to the next farm. Dinky is curious about the new places and animals she sees. Ducks quack and waddle around the barnyard. Big spotted pigs grunt and gobble up scraps of food the neighbor feeds them.

Then Dinky hears the sound of a horse neighing. The farmer leads Dinky to a stable.

Inside, Dinky sees a horse with a bandage on its side. The horse has cut himself on a fence. The horse is scared and very nervous. He paws the ground in his stall, snorting and shaking his head.

Dinky will keep the horse company and calm the horse down. She must make sure the horse does not move around too much. The horse could hurt himself even more if he bumps his cut. Once the horse is calm his cut will heal faster.

Farm Donkey

Farm Donkey

When the horse is well enough to be alone again, the farmer comes back to get Dinky. As the farmer leads Dinky home, it begins to snow. The soft, wet snowflakes cover Dinky's fur. She hurries back home to her nice, dry shed.

All through the night the snow keeps falling. In the morning Dinky hears the farmer's children shouting and laughing. She pokes her head out of the shed and takes one step forward. Her front hoof sinks into the snow. Dinky hurries back into the shed. She does not like snow any better than she likes mud.

The farmer's children bring Dinky some carrots and try to coax her out into the snow. They want her to give them a sleigh ride. Dinky sniffs the carrots. She wants to play with the children, but she does not want to walk in the snow.

Farm Stories

The snow has caused many problems. It has made the roads dangerous for travel. The farmer's neighbor is out of feed. His animals are hungry, but he cannot drive to the feed store. The snow is too deep and the roads are too slippery.

The farmer will lend some feed to his neighbor, but he needs Dinky's help to get there. The farmer calls to Dinky as he walks to her shed.

The farmer stamps down the snow in front of the shed for her. When Dinky walks out, she does not sink in the packed snow!

The farmer loads sacks of feed for his neighbor onto the sleigh. Then he hitches the sleigh to Dinky's harness. Walking ahead of her, he stamps down the snow as they move very slowly out the gate toward the neighbor's house.

Farm Donkey

Up on the road the neighbor waits with his horse and cart. Dinky has saved the day!

Back home Dinky sees the children and trots over to them. Dinky is very happy to see them. She is ready to give the children a sleigh ride now!

Little Calf

Illustrated by Debbie Pinkney
Written by Lenaya Raack
and Lisa Harkrader

The snow falls gently outside the barn. Inside, the animals are safe and dry. It is nighttime on the farm. In the dim light hens cluck and settle down on their nests high up in the rafters. The horses close their eyes and give a last whinny before they fall asleep.

In a far corner a lantern glows like a firefly in the growing darkness. A young boy watches Mother Cow, who is lying quietly on her side in the hay. It is time for her calf to be born.

Soon a sleepy calf lies beside Mother Cow. The calf's fur is wet and matted, but the boy thinks she is the most beautiful calf he has ever seen.

"I will name you Daisy," he tells the calf.

Daisy sits quietly as Mother Cow cleans the calf's wet fur. Soon Daisy is clean and dry.

Little Calf

Little Calf

    Daisy is only fifteen minutes old, but that is old enough to start learning the things a calf needs to know. The boy watches as Mother Cow gives Daisy a gentle nudge. It is time for Daisy to stand.

    The little calf is still weak, and her legs want to move in all different directions. Daisy rises up on her back legs, but her front legs tremble, and she falls into the hay. Then Daisy pushes up on her front legs, and her back legs topple out from under her. When Daisy finally stands, her legs are very wobbly.

    Now that she is standing, Daisy wants to eat. She is hungry. Daisy needs to drink her mother's milk to grow stronger. She moves a little closer to her mother's side. Mother Cow can give milk now that Daisy has been born. Daisy finds Mother Cow's udder and begins to drink the nourishing milk.

Farm Stories

When Daisy is a little older, the boy opens the barn door. Daisy steps into the cool spring air for the first time. She blinks her eyes at the bright sun. A dragonfly flits in front of Daisy's nose. She is not sure what to make of this odd creature. Daisy shakes her head and chases it around the barnyard. She watches as it flies off into the sky.

Daisy hears something new and turns to look. It is a mother pig and her babies. The baby pigs are called piglets. They are smaller than Daisy, but they are very noisy! They squeal and grunt as they trot around inside their pen.

Daisy wanders near the fence and sniffs the white flowers. Then she tries to reach the grass just beyond the wooden posts. Daisy tries to squeeze under the fence, but she is too big.

Little Calf

Little Calf

Daisy is hungry again. Now that she is older she does not drink Mother Cow's milk. Daisy drinks powdered milk and water. The boy brings it to her twice a day. He puts it in an oversized bottle, and Daisy drinks out of it.

The boy loves Daisy. Each day, between chores, he comes to pet her. He pats Daisy on her back and scratches her neck, and Daisy nuzzles up against him. The boy wants to take Daisy to the county fair. He tells Daisy that she will be the best calf at the fair. He thinks she can win a ribbon.

They must work hard. There are many things for Daisy to learn. She has to learn how to stay calm around people and around lots of noise. Daisy also has to learn to follow the boy and listen to what he tells her to do.

At first Daisy does not understand what they must do to get ready for the fair. She likes to walk with the boy, but not today. Daisy wants to stay in the barn.

The boy knows it is important to practice every day. He pulls on the rope to get Daisy to move. The boy leads Daisy out of the barnyard.

They walk to a nearby field. "Stop," he tells her, but Daisy keeps moving. She wants to look at a rabbit peeking out from a bush. The boy leans against Daisy and pushes hard. Finally, she stops.

"Now start," he calls, but Daisy wants to stay. She likes chewing on the tender grass and standing under the shady trees. But the boy digs his heels into the ground and then pulls on the reins with all his might. Finally, Daisy stops eating and follows as the boy leads her across the field.

Little Calf

Daisy will need to look her very best when she goes to the fair. Her coat must be clean and her hair cut just right. The boy leads Daisy out of the barn and into the pen. It is time to practice giving her a bath. Daisy likes the cool water squirting out of the hose. She stands quietly while the boy scrubs her with a brush. He washes away all the dust and mud and pieces of hay.

The boy dries off Daisy and steps back to admire her nice clean coat. All that is left for him to do now is to give Daisy a haircut. The boy brings out the clippers. Daisy stands very still while the boy trims her coat and tail.

The boy is sure that Daisy is the best-looking calf ever!

"You are ready for the fair," he tells her.

Farm Stories

The fair is a big, colorful, noisy place. Smiling people are walking everywhere. Children ride the Ferris wheel and play games to win prizes. People eat corn on the cob and cotton candy. Others look at the prize-winning pies that people have baked or at the food they have grown.

Daisy is staying in a big barn where there are many calves and cows. Daisy will have her own stall. Daisy and the boy rush to the barn so they can prepare for the big competition.

There are many barns at the fair. Daisy and the boy pass chickens, ducks, and sheep. In the barn next to Daisy's barn, the pigs oink as boys and girls get ready for the competition, too. The horses neigh in the next barn, and sheep baa as boys and girls trim their wool. Everyone is nervous.

Little Calf

The boy finds the stall that has Daisy's name on it. He leads her inside. Daisy moves restlessly in her stall. She can tell something is different today. Boys and girls rush all around to get their calves ready for the judging.

Daisy must look her best today. The boy brings out the combs, brushes, and shampoo. He hooks up the water hose and sets out the dryer.

First, Daisy gets a bath. The boy scrubs her with the brush and cleans all the mud from her hooves. Then the boy brushes Daisy until her coat shines brightly. Then he clips some of the hair around her head. Finally, he trims the hair on Daisy's tail and fluffs the end of her tail into a puffy ball. Now she is ready for her new leather halter. And it is time for the competition to begin!

The boy leads Daisy into the ring. Many other boys and girls lead their calves into the ring, too. Daisy knows what to do. There are lots of people and lots of noise at the fair, but Daisy stays calm. She follows the boy just as he has taught her. When he stops, Daisy stops. When he says turn, she turns.

Daisy and the other calves line up now, nose to tail. The judges watch Daisy to see how well she minds the boy. The judges walk past the calves and look at each one carefully.

Now the calves are side by side. With the boy's help, Daisy carefully lines up her feet. They stand proudly as the judges check Daisy's ears, lift her tail, and feel her coat. Now they walk around the ring one last time. The judges decide which calf is the best. They say it is Daisy!

Daisy is back in her stall in the barn. Her ribbon hangs on the gate in front of her. People stop to look at the prize-winning calf.

Everyone admires Daisy and wants to pet her. They all crowd around Daisy and wish that someday they might have a calf just like her. They tell the boy what a wonderful job he did raising Daisy to be a champion calf.

The boy talks to them and tells them how proud he is of Daisy. He says she worked very hard to win the competition. He tells them how he and Daisy practiced every day.

"Your hard work paid off," a man says. "She is the blue-ribbon calf!"

"Yes, she is," says the boy as he scratches Daisy's head. "I knew it all along!"

Little Calf

Little Boy Blue

This Little Pig Went to Market

Baby Pig

Illustrated by Kathy Rusynyk
Written by Lenaya Raack
and Lisa Harkrader

A pair of big brown eyes peek through the fence in the barn. They belong to a little girl who lives on the farm. Her name is Penny.

Penny kneels in the hay and watches Mother Pig feed her new litter of piglets. The girl stays quiet. She does not want to scare Mother Pig or her new babies. Penny starts to count the tiny tails—one, two, three . . . all the way up to nine.

Penny gets up and quietly moves around to the other side of Mother Pig. Now Penny can see all of the piglets. They are all perfectly pink—except for the littlest one on the end. The littlest pig has brown spots all over her body.

This piglet is Penny's favorite. "I'll call you Baby Pig," says Penny. "You will be my special pet."

Baby Pig

Baby Pig

Baby Pig moves with her family to a new home. It is called a sty, or pigpen. The sty has hay on the ground and a fence around it to keep the piglets from wandering off.

Baby Pig lives here with her sisters and brothers and Mother Pig. At night the piglets sleep close to each other to stay warm. Sometimes they even sleep on top of one another. The sty looks like a pig pile.

Today, Baby Pig wakes up first. She sniffs the ground looking for food. She is hungry all the time, but this morning there is nothing in the sty to eat.

Suddenly, Baby Pig hears Penny coming. Baby Pig watches the girl pour some food into a long wooden bucket called a trough. Now all of the pigs are awake. Baby Pig has to push past the other hungry pigs to eat.

Farm Stories

Today, Baby Pig and her family are going into the barnyard with the other animals. Baby Pig likes the barnyard because it is much bigger than the sty. There is more room for her to run and play. There are new animals for Baby Pig to see.

The girl opens the gate of the pigpen. One by one the piglets follow their mother into the barnyard. A curious calf comes up to sniff Baby Pig. Baby Pig does not mind. She wants to play, but Mother Pig grunts loudly, and the calf moves away.

Baby Pig walks over to the fence, sniffing the ground for food. Penny comes over. She holds her hand behind her back. "Are you hungry, Baby Pig?" asks Penny. "Here is a treat for you." Penny pulls her hand from behind her back. She is holding an apple. Penny gives the apple to Baby Pig.

Baby Pig

Baby Pig

It is summertime on the farm, and it is very hot. The ground is dry and dusty. In the shade of the barn, the chickens roll in the dust to keep their feathers from sticking together.

Baby Pig does not sweat, so she needs to roll in the mud to get cool. It has not rained in a very long time, though. There is no mud in the pigpen!

Soon Penny brings out a hose and makes a big mud hole by squirting water on the dirt. Baby Pig is the first one to jump in. She rolls and wriggles and splashes until she is covered in mud. Baby Pig is not hot anymore.

The other pigs follow Baby Pig. They run and jump into the mud, too. Soon all the pigs are the color of mud. Penny laughs. "I can hardly see you in all that mud," she says.

Baby Pig is looking for something good to eat. She walks over to where the chickens are eating, but she does not want to eat grain. She walks over to where the cows are eating, but she does not want to eat hay.

Maybe there is something good to eat in the barn. Baby Pig sees a pail. She knows Penny sometimes carries food to the pigpen in a pail. Baby Pig sticks her head in the pail, but it is empty. She tries to pull her head out, but the pail will not come off. Baby Pig is stuck!

Baby Pig shakes her head, but the pail does not move. She begins to run. The chickens and roosters see Baby Pig and run away. The geese see her, too. They honk and fly up on the fence.

Splash! Baby Pig lands in the mud. Finally, the pail pops off!

Baby Pig

Baby Pig

Sometimes Penny takes Baby Pig for walks. Today they are going for a short walk down the road. Baby Pig likes to go for walks because there are lots of new things for her to see.

Baby Pig watches a squirrel run up a tree. She sees a rabbit hop into a bush. Baby Pig wiggles her nose when a butterfly flutters past.

Baby Pig stops to smell the bright, yellow flowers that grow along the road. As Penny and Baby Pig walk farther up the road, they see a large flock of sheep. Dogs are herding the sheep into a field.

Baby Pig wants to help herd the sheep, but Penny tells her, "No, Baby Pig, pigs do not herd sheep."

They stop under an apple tree to rest. Penny feeds Baby Pig an apple for being so good. Apples are Baby Pig's favorite snack.

Farm Stories

Baby Pig is hungry again. She sees corn growing on cornstalks in the field. Baby Pig loves the corn that Penny pours into the pig trough. She thinks corn growing in a field must taste even better.

Baby Pig squeezes under the fence and races for the big cornstalks. She knocks over a cornstalk and eats the ears of corn.

Soon Baby Pig sees a rabbit hopping around the cornstalks. Baby Pig trots after it. She chases the rabbit up and down the rows of corn. Baby Pig wants to play, but the rabbit disappears down a hole. Now Baby Pig is lost. The corn is too tall! Baby Pig cannot see the barnyard.

Then Baby Pig hears something familiar. It is Penny's voice! Baby Pig squeals, and Penny comes running to find her.

Baby Pig

Baby Pig

Baby Pig is five months old now. She is too big to be picked up and carried by Penny. But Baby Pig likes to follow Penny around the barnyard while the little girl does her chores. She watches as Penny throws grain on the ground and the chickens gobble it up. Baby Pig trots into the henhouse with Penny and watches her carefully gather the eggs.

Then Baby Pig follows Penny into the barn. Penny climbs up a ladder into the hayloft. She throws hay down to the barn floor to feed the cows. Penny does not notice the hay falling on top of Baby Pig.

Baby Pig is covered in hay! When Penny sees the pig in the hay, she giggles playfully and says, "Sorry, Baby Pig."

Baby Pig wiggles and shakes, and the hay falls to the floor of the barn.

The farm is quiet. It is nighttime now. In the barn, the cows sleepily eat one last mouthful of hay. The calves are already curled up in their stalls, fast asleep. The hens are sitting on their nests in the henhouse. Their chicks are safely tucked under their mothers' feathers. Outside, the pigs are back in their sty. They are lying down and getting ready to sleep, too. They crowd together to keep warm.

One pig is still awake, though. It is Baby Pig, the little girl's special pet. Baby Pig and Penny sit on the bottom step of the porch. They watch the fireflies blinking on and off in the darkness. The barnyard is dark and empty. The farmhouse is quiet.

When it is time for bed, Penny walks Baby Pig back to her pen and gives her a good-night hug. Baby Pig curls up to sleep with her brothers and sisters.

Baby Pig

Farm Stories

Baby Pig

Now Baby Pig is one year old. She is not the littlest pig on the farm anymore. Baby Pig has been eating and growing, and now she is a big pig. Soon Baby Pig will have her own babies.

Some things have not changed, though. Baby Pig still likes to eat. She likes apples and corn and scraps from the farmhouse. Baby Pig still likes to roll in the mud on hot days, too.

And Baby Pig is still Penny's special pet. Every day Penny brings her food and stops to talk to her. The little girl scratches Baby Pig on the head and gives her a hug. Penny is excited that Baby Pig will soon be having babies of her own.

When the new piglets are born, Penny chooses one to be her new pet. She knows this piglet is just as special as Baby Pig.

Oats, Peas, Beans, and Barley Grow

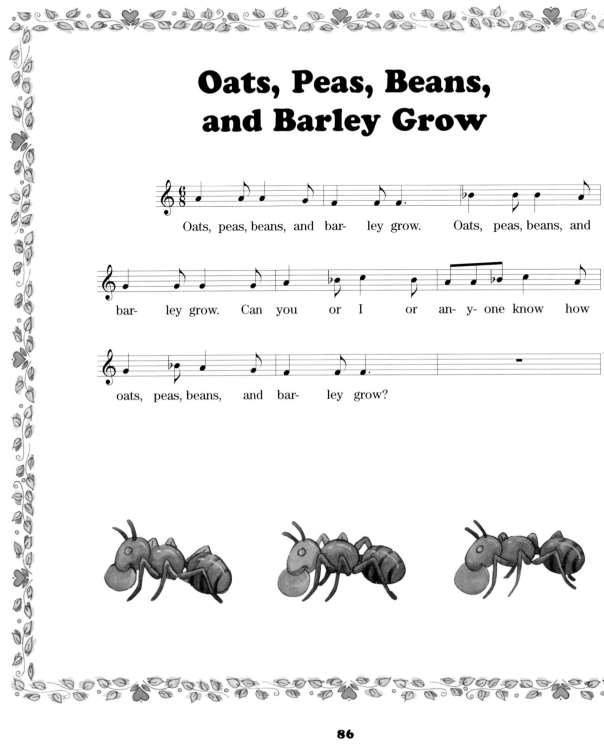

Oats, peas, beans, and bar- ley grow. Oats, peas, beans, and

bar- ley grow. Can you or I or an- y- one know how

oats, peas, beans, and bar- ley grow?

Oats, Peas, Beans, and Barley Grow

Hickory Dickory Dock

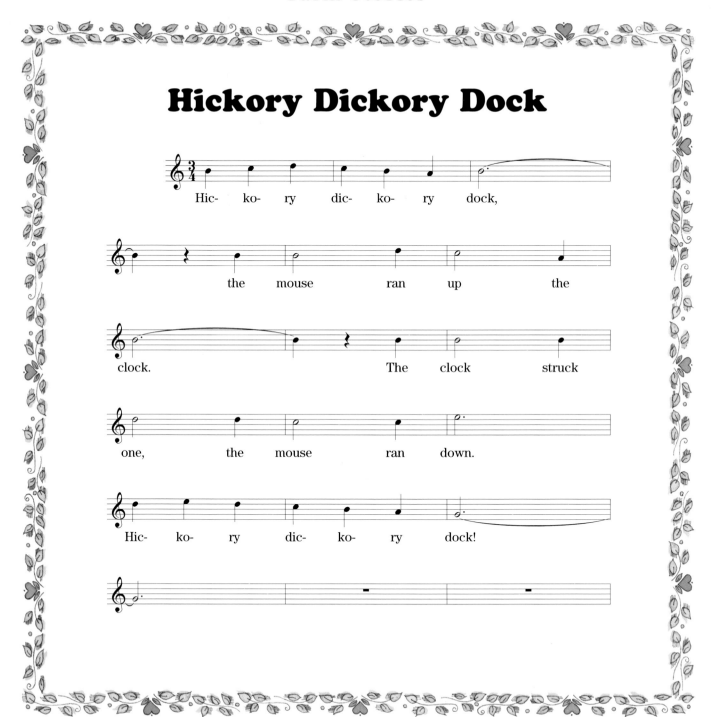

Fluffy Chick

Illustrated by Kathy Wilburn
Written by Brian Conway

Fluffy Chick woke up before dawn. Her tiny tummy told her it was time for breakfast, but her parents said it was still too early.

"Why don't you go back to sleep, Fluffy?" said Mother Hen. "Farmer John will have our breakfast ready soon."

"But I am hungry now," peeped little Fluffy Chick.

Mother Hen nudged Red Rooster. "Will you bring Fluffy a snack?" she asked.

"I have to hurry off to work," said Red Rooster. "I cannot be late for the sunrise!"

"May I go out to the barnyard to find myself a snack?" Fluffy asked her parents.

Fluffy Chick

Fluffy Chick

"I suppose you are old enough now," said Mother Hen. "But be careful, and do not stray too far."

Fluffy Chick hopped out to the barnyard. She heard the piglets sloshing around in their bath.

"Excuse me, friends," said Fluffy Chick. "Do you know where I can find an early morning snack?"

"It is bathtime now," giggled Penny Piglet. "We never eat until breakfast is ready."

Fluffy Chick hopped over to the dairy. "Good morning, Mother Cow," she said cheerily. "Do you know where I can find a snack?"

"Would you like a few drops of milk?" asked Mother Cow.

"Oh, thank you," said Fluffy. "But I cannot drink milk. I will see what else I can find."

Fluffy went to see her little friends, the barnyard mice. "Wake up, friends," Fluffy Chick peeped, "and help me find a morning snack."

"Why don't you have a sip of water and go back to bed?" yawned Missy Mouse.

Fluffy followed her sleepy friend out to the well. They shared a little drink of water. Fluffy Chick was not thirsty at all. Her tummy wanted something more.

"Thank you, Missy," said Fluffy, "but I am still much too hungry to wait for breakfast."

"Come with me," Missy Mouse said. "I will show you where the mice go when we want to have a midnight snack."

Fluffy Chick

Fluffy Chick

Missy Mouse scurried across the barnyard. She ran into the stable, and Fluffy hurried in after her.

"Look at these juicy red apples!" Missy Mouse called to Fluffy. "Mother Mare likes to share her snacks with us."

"I have more apples than I can eat," said Mother Mare. "Come have a bite, Fluffy."

Fluffy tapped one apple with her tiny beak. She did not taste a thing. Fluffy pecked again, and she hopped back as the pile came tumbling down.

"Oh dear," she said. "I am afraid this snack is too much for a little chick like me."

"Why don't you find some sweet berries in the meadow?" said Mother Mare.

On her way through the meadow, Fluffy found Betty Bunny. Betty was gathering blueberries, and she rolled one over to Fluffy. "Why don't you try one?" said Betty.

"Thank you, Betty," said Fluffy. "The berries do look like a sweet snack!"

Fluffy tapped the berry with her beak, and it rolled away from her. Fluffy Chick did not taste a thing. She pecked the blueberry harder this time. The berry bounced and rolled away again.

Betty Bunny laughed. "You have to hold on to a blueberry when it is as plump as this one," she said. "I think a little chick like you needs a smaller snack."

Fluffy Chick

Fluffy Chick

On her way back to the barnyard, Fluffy met Lucy Ladybug. "What is the matter, Fluffy?" asked Lucy.

"I am very hungry," said Fluffy Chick. "But all the sweet snacks on the farm are too big for me!"

Lucy Ladybug knew a tiny farm friend who could help. She brought Fluffy to visit Barney Bumblebee. "What is your favorite early morning snack?" Fluffy asked Barney.

"We sip sweet nectar from the wildflowers," Barney said. "Would you like to try some?"

Fluffy pressed her beak into the soft flower's petals. She did not taste a thing. "I am afraid it is not the best snack for a little chick like me," said Fluffy.

"I know where to find a good snack for you!" Barney Bumblebee buzzed.

Fluffy Chick followed Barney to a spot beside the garden. Barney hovered over a big brown sack. "Here it is," he said. "Farmer John takes one out to the chicken coop every morning."

"This cannot be a snack for me," said Fluffy Chick. "It is much too big, and it does not look very tasty."

She pecked her beak against the side of the food sack. She tasted something dry and dusty.

"Yuck!" said Fluffy Chick. "This does not taste very good at all! It tastes like something old Billie Goat would eat!"

Fluffy Chick

Mother Hen spotted her hungry chick shuffling across the barnyard. "Fluffy!" she called. "Didn't you hear your father calling? You are late for breakfast!"

Fluffy Chick hurried over to the breakfast Farmer John had set out. She pecked up the tiny bits of grain as quickly as she could, and each one tasted even better than the last.

"Barney Bumblebee was right!" Fluffy Chick told her mother. "A breakfast like this one is the best early morning snack for a little chick like me!"

Baby Bunny

Illustrated by Deborah Colvin Borgo
Written by Lisa Harkrader

Baby Bunny hopped across the meadow. "I get to go by myself!" she called happily as she stopped at Woodchuck's hole. "Did you hear me, Woodchuck?"

Her friend Woodchuck popped up from his hole. "Of course I heard you," he said.

"I am going to the garden to gather carrots for lunch," said Baby Bunny. "My mother says I am old enough now."

"You might need some help," said Woodchuck. "I can go with you."

"No," said Baby Bunny. "I am grown up now. I can do it myself." And she hopped off on her way to the garden.

Baby Bunny

Baby Bunny

At least she thought it was toward the garden.

The garden was always easy to find when she was with her mother. But now that she was by herself, Baby Bunny was not sure which way to turn.

"Where are you going?" asked a small voice. It was Baby Bunny's friend Caterpillar.

"I am going to gather carrots for lunch," said Baby Bunny.

"I want to go with you," said Caterpillar.

"No," said Baby Bunny. "I am grown up now. I can do it myself."

And she hopped through the trees, hoping she would find the garden soon.

Baby Bunny hopped and hopped, and soon she came to a pond. She could not go forward. Rabbits cannot swim. She did not know which way to turn.

Her friend Frog leaped from the water onto a lily pad. "Where are you going?" he asked.

"To gather carrots," said Baby Bunny.

Her friend Chirp flitted down from the sky and landed beside her. "We will go with you," said Chirp.

"Yes," said Frog. "We can help you."

Baby Bunny shook her head. She did not want her friends to think she was too little to find the garden without help. "No," said Baby Bunny. "I have to go by myself."

Baby Bunny

Baby Bunny

Baby Bunny stared across the water, and there was the garden! But it was on the other side of the pond.

"I cannot swim," said Baby Bunny. "But I will hop from lily pad to lily pad until I reach the other side."

She leaped onto the closest lily pad, and it began to move! It was not a lily pad at all. It was her friend Turtle. "I will take you across on my back," he said.

"But I told everyone I could do it myself," said Baby Bunny.

"You did," said Turtle. "You found the garden all by yourself. Now you will gather carrots and take them back home by yourself."

Turtle swam all the way across the pond with Baby Bunny on his back. Baby Bunny climbed off when they reached the other side.

"Thank you, Turtle," she said as she hopped to the garden to pick a crisp, fat carrot from the dirt.

Chirp flew down and landed on the scarecrow. "I can see everything when I am flying way up in the sky," said Chirp. "When you finish picking carrots I can help you find a shorter way to get home."

"Good idea," said Baby Bunny. "Even bunnies who can do things themselves need good friends to help them out sometimes."

Mary Had a Little Lamb

Ma- ry had a lit- tle lamb, lit- tle lamb, lit- tle lamb.

Ma- ry had a lit- tle lamb, its fleece was white as snow.

Ev- 'rywhere that Ma- ry went, Ma- ry went, Ma- ry went,

Ev- 'rywhere that Ma- ry went, the lamb was sure to go.

Six Little Ducks

Six lit-tle ducks that I once knew, Fat ones, skin-ny ones,

fair ones, too. But the one lit-tle duck with the feather on his back,

he led the others with a quack, quack, quack! Quack, quack, quack!

Quack, quack, quack! He led the others with a quack, quack, quack!

Little Quack

Illustrated by Kurt Mitchell
Written by Sarah Toast

It was Little Quack's first day on the pond. There were so many things to see! Little Quack stopped again and again as he swam in a line with his family.

"Little Quack, go to the back!" his sisters said. "You are holding up the line."

"Okay," said Little Quack.

Little Quack did not mind going to the back of the line. It gave him more time to explore.

When his family walked through the reeds, Little Quack peeked around them. When his family looked straight ahead, Little Quack looked up at the trees.

Little Quack

When his family swam on the water, Little Quack dipped under it. When a creature under the water blew bubbles, Little Quack blew some back.

His family kept paddling along. Little Quack did not notice they were swimming away. They did not seem to notice that Little Quack stayed behind to play and explore.

When Little Quack popped up above the surface again, he did not see his family. Little Quack looked around. All of the new things at the pond seemed a little scary now. Little Quack would feel better if his family were here. How would he find them?

Little Quack paddled in a slow circle. A strange green animal with a loud, deep voice watched him. As a fly buzzed past, the strange green animal's tongue shot out. Z-z-zip! He caught the fly.

The green animal laughed as Little Quack started to back up quickly. "Do not worry, ducky," the animal said. "I am a frog. I eat bugs, not ducks."

That made Little Quack feel better. "Hello, Frog," he said. "Have you seen my family?"

"I only look for flies, not ducks," croaked Frog. "You should ask Bluebird. She sees everything."

"Bluebird?" Little Quack thought to himself. He had never heard of a bluebird. His mother had some blue feathers, but the rest of her was a lovely brown. Little Quack wished that he could see his mother's feathers right now.

"I guess I will keep looking," said Little Quack.

As he paddled along, Little Quack saw blue feathers. He hurried toward them.

But it was not his mother. It was the bluebird! Little Quack stared at her. She looked different, but pretty.

"Hello, little one," Bluebird chirped.

"No, my name is Little Quack," the duckling said.

Bluebird laughed. "Where is your family, Little Quack?" she asked.

"I don't know," said Little Quack. "Frog says that you can help me find them."

"Wait here," said Bluebird. "I will look."

Bluebird flew off, but she was not gone for long. She landed on a cattail near Little Quack.

"Did you find them?" asked Little Quack.

Little Quack

"Your family is just over there," Bluebird said as she pointed with her wing.

Little Quack followed her directions and paddled off. But the shore all looked the same to him now.

Little Quack could not find his mother and he could not see the bluebird. And worst of all, a very strange animal was watching him from the shore!

Little Quack backed away as the animal got closer and closer to the water.

"Hi there!" the animal called. "Were you born this spring, too?"

Little Quack stopped. "I was hatched, not born," he said. "Who are you?"

The animal laughed. "I am Fox Kit."

"Why don't you have feathers?" asked Little Quack.

"Foxes have fur instead of feathers," said Fox Kit.

"Poor Fox Kit," Little Quack thought to himself. "It must be hard not to have feathers."

"Everyone in my family has feathers," said Little Quack. "If you want, we could all give you some. But first I have to find my family."

Little Quack

Fox Kit smiled. He did not seem strange anymore. "That's all right," he said. "I think I saw your family on the other side of these weeds."

"Thank you," said Little Quack.

Little Quack swam as fast as he could. He did not stop to explore, or look up at the trees, or take a dip under the water. He went straight to the other side of the weeds, and there was his family!

"Mother!" Little Quack called out. He was so happy to finally see his mother and his sisters.

Little Quack splashed and paddled as fast as he could to get to his mother. His mother paddled toward Little Quack and lifted her wing. Little Quack swam underneath it and nuzzled against his mother's fine feathers.

"I didn't know where you were," said Little Quack. "I was looking all over for you."

"I always knew where you were, Little Quack," said his mother. "I kept my eye on you all the time and never lost sight of you. And I never will. For you are my Little Quack."

Bingo

There was a far-mer had a dog, and

Bing- o was his name- o. B- I- N- G- O!

B- I- N- G- O! B- I- N- G- O! And

Bing- o was his name- o!

Bingo

Oh, Where Has My Little Dog Gone

Oh, where, oh, where, has my lit- tle dog gone? Oh, where, oh, where can he be? With his ears cut short, and his tail cut long, oh, where, oh, where can he be?

Farm Puppy

Illustrated by Deborah Colvin Borgo
Written by Lenaya Raack

Farm Stories

In a corner of the barn, four tiny puppies snuggle safely against Mother Dog's side. The puppies are only four days old.

Mother Dog made a bed for them away from the clucking hens, away from the curious piglets, and away from the busy farmer.

The tiny puppies sleep most of the day. They cannot see, they cannot hear, and they cannot walk. The puppies need Mother Dog to feed them and take care of them.

Every day the puppies drink Mother Dog's milk, and Mother Dog gives her babies a bath. And every night Father Dog sleeps near them.

During the day, Father Dog helps the farmer take care of his sheep.

Farm Puppy

The farmer watches one of the puppies explore the barn. His name is Farm Puppy, and he is three weeks old now.

Farm Puppy can see and hear all the animals who live in the barn. He hears the rooster crow every morning. He sees the brown hen sitting on her eggs. He hears the piglets squealing as they play. And he sees the brown cow eating the hay.

Today, Farm Puppy visits the baby chicks. Farm Puppy wants to round up the chicks. He walks in a circle around the chicks, trying to move them to the back of the barn.

When Farm Puppy comes too close to the chicks, they run and hide under Mother Hen's feathers. Mother Hen squawks at Farm Puppy, and he runs back to Mother Dog.

Farm Stories

The bright sun shines down on the barnyard. It is now springtime!

Farm Puppy is five weeks old. He likes to watch his mother and father herd the sheep. Father Dog herds the sheep through a gate. Mother Dog chases after a sheep that is running away.

Soon Farm Puppy will be able to herd sheep, too. For now he practices with some of the other animals in the barnyard.

Farm Puppy runs over to the chickens, but they keep eating. He races over to Mother Pig and her piglets. Mother Pig just snorts at Farm Puppy. She does not want anyone near her piglets.

Farm Puppy runs over to the calves, but they just keep eating, too. No one seems to want to listen to Farm Puppy.

Farm Stories

Farm Puppy

Now Farm Puppy is six weeks old. He finally gets to help the farmer, Mother Dog, and Father Dog take the sheep to the pasture!

Farm Puppy follows Mother and Father Dog as they move the sheep out through the farm gate. The farmer blows his whistle and moves his hands.

When the farmer moves his hands, Father Dog starts to walk around the sheep. When the farmer blows his whistle, Mother Dog barks at the sheep and makes them move.

Now Farm Puppy plays follow the leader. When Mother Dog runs after the sheep, Farm Puppy runs after the sheep, too. When Father Dog lies down and stares at the sheep, so does Farm Puppy.

"This is good practice for being a sheepdog!" thinks Farm Puppy.

Farm Stories

Farm Puppy has been exploring the pasture while the sheep eat. It is hot in the sun. Farm Puppy looks for some water to drink.

In the corner of the pasture he finds a pond. Farm Puppy bends his head to take a drink. Suddenly, he sees a strange dog in the water!

Farm Puppy lies on the ground and stares. But the dog has gone away. Farm Puppy stands up again. He sees the dog again!

Then Farm Puppy barks at the strange dog. The other dog barks, too. Farm Puppy circles the pond. But the dog still stares back.

Farm Puppy runs toward the dog and then— splash! Farm Puppy is all wet.

The farmer rescues Farm Puppy and takes him back to the herd.

Farm Puppy

Farm Puppy

Farm Puppy is staying home today. He likes to play in the barnyard. Farm Puppy walks up to the geese and stares at them.

He is trying to herd them into the barn. But the geese just stare back! When they walk away from the barn, Farm Puppy tries to stop them. He circles them and barks loudly.

Honk! Honk! Honk! The geese run in all different directions! Farm Puppy races after them, into the squawking chickens, over the hay bales, through the legs of the mooing calves, under the fence, and back again.

Then the geese fly on top of a hay wagon. Farm Puppy stops and barks, but they will not come down. And they will not go into the barn.

"Herding is hard work!" thinks Farm Puppy.

Suddenly, Farm Puppy hears another kind of honk. The children have come back home on the big, yellow school bus!

Farm Puppy races to meet them. The bus starts to move, and Farm Puppy starts to chase it. But the bus is too fast for him to catch.

"Here, Puppy!" the children yell. Farm Puppy runs to them as they walk toward the house. But Farm Puppy does not want them to go into the house. He circles the children. The children stop.

"Puppy must think we are some kind of funny sheep," the boy says.

When Farm Puppy sits and stares, the children start walking. When Farm Puppy stands and barks, they stop. Finally, they tell Farm Puppy to sit and be a good dog.

Farm Puppy

Farm Puppy

Just then, Farm Puppy hears the farmer's whistle. The farmer is calling him!

Farm Puppy is now six months old. The farmer must teach Farm Puppy what to do to become a good sheepdog. They practice every day. Farm Puppy learns what to do when the farmer whistles and moves his hands.

Farm Puppy learns how to take the sheep out through the gate and bring them back in again. Farm Puppy learns to move the sheep so that he is on one side of them and the farmer is on the other side. The farmer also teaches Farm Puppy what to do when a sheep runs away.

Farm Puppy learns very fast. Soon, Farm Puppy will be able to move the sheep just like his mother and father.

Farm Stories

Today, Farm Puppy and Father Dog are out in the pasture with the sheep. The sky darkens, and rain begins to fall. They hear sounds of thunder, and the farmer decides it is time to take the sheep back to the farm to be safe.

The sheep are very afraid. They start to run away. Farm Puppy circles the sheep like his father. Then the farmer gives a signal.

Now Farm Puppy and Father Dog must turn the sheep. The sheep head for the farm.

When the thunder roars again, one lamb runs away. Farm Puppy remembers what he was taught and runs after it.

Father Dog and the farmer take the sheep back to the farm. They wait for Farm Puppy to come home with the lamb.

Farm Puppy

Finally, the farmer and Father Dog go looking for Farm Puppy and the lamb. There is no sign of them. Father Dog barks. Then Farm Puppy barks back.

The farmer and Father Dog run to Farm Puppy. They find Farm Puppy and the lamb. The lamb is stuck in mud, and the farmer pulls him out. He pats Farm Puppy and tells him he is the best sheepdog.

Goat Kids

Illustrated by Andrea Tachiera
Written by Catherine McCafferty
and Brian Conway

Farm Stories

Goat twins Billy and Nanny stand up from their bed of hay when the barn door swings open. The farmer always comes into the barn very early in the morning to milk the mama goat.

Today, when the farmer finishes with the milking, he walks over to pat Nanny and Billy.

"You two will have to look after yourselves today," the farmer says. "I have another job for your mother."

He leads their mother away. Mama Goat will help to care for a newborn lamb whose own mother cannot take care of it.

What will Billy and Nanny do today? Without their mother there, the two goat kids can do whatever they like. Billy likes to eat. Nanny likes to jump and climb. But they also like to stay together.

Goat Kids

Billy and Nanny nibble happily from the hay bin. They have both had their teeth since the day they were born. And that is a good thing since Billy likes to eat all the time!

Nanny ventures out to the barnyard. There is more hay and grass to eat along the high barnyard fence, but Nanny feels like climbing. Suddenly, she sees that the shed roof is just the right height for climbing.

Nanny hops onto a hay bale, then leans her front hooves against the shed and jumps up.

Soon Billy comes out to the barnyard. He sees his sister in a high place on the shed roof.

Billy hops and jumps to join Nanny on the shed. Their two-toed feet and sturdy hooves keep them sure-footed. Though they are only kids, they have strong legs and good balance, like all goats do.

Nanny and Billy look around the farm from the top of the shed roof. They see the pigs and the chickens back in the barnyard. Those animals could never climb so high. Nanny and Billy like being up high, in a spot where they can see everything.

High places are good lookout spots for goats. If mountain goats think danger is coming, they spread out and climb to high places. That way, they see any approaching enemies before the enemies see them. Then, if they have to, they can leap down to surprise their enemies from different directions.

But there is nothing dangerous to see on the farm. Billy and Nanny climb for fun and for practice.

Billy sees something new. The roof slopes down into the farmer's yard! Billy thinks that he might find a snack there!

Goat Kids

Goat Kids

After climbing carefully down the other side of the roof, Billy and Nanny land feet-first in the farmer's yard. Goats have thick padding inside their hooves. Their "shock absorbers" are in the inside layers of their feet. They help to keep Billy and Nanny from hurting their legs when they land after jumping.

Billy stops at the farmer's kitchen door. He climbs the three little steps to the back porch and waits for the door to open. Nanny climbs up the steps, then down again. She does this a few times, then goes to find a higher place to climb.

When Nanny gets to the farmer's pickup truck, she jumps onto the hood and then onto the next tallest spot, on the truck's roof. She climbs the same way mountain goats do, as if she is jumping from one narrow ledge to another.

Suddenly, Billy sees the farmer enter his yard. The farmer chuckles when he sees Billy on the steps and Nanny on the truck.

"Okay, you two," the farmer says, "I have a better place for two busy kids like you."

The farmer leads Billy and Nanny to a big field. The field is covered with bushes and thick brush. Other goats are already munching on the heavy undergrowth. Billy sees delicious food everywhere he looks.

Billy's first feeding stop is a thick, prickly bush. Billy expects the plant to be tender, but his tough mouth feels prickles instead. If Billy's mother was with him she would eat the toughest parts of the plant and leave the tender parts for Billy and Nanny. Billy does the best he can to get at the tender parts.

Goat Kids

Billy is so busy eating that he does not notice Nanny wandering off. Since there are so many other goats around, Nanny does not mind being a little further away from Billy. Nanny tries to run and leap through the field, but she bumps into one goat after another. The field is too crowded for the kind of jumping that Nanny likes to do.

At the far end of the field, Nanny sees a fence. She trots toward it. The fence does not look too high. Nanny steps back for a running start. She jumps and sails over the fence in one leap! Nanny lands in a soft, grassy field. Then she jumps back into the brushy field. Then back over the fence again!

Getting over the fence is easy for a good jumper like Nanny. When she has jumped enough, Nanny settles down to munch for a while in the grassy field.

Nanny does not see the herd of cows munching nearby in the grassy field. But then she hears a loud "Mooooooo!" Nanny crouches low to the ground when she hears heavy footsteps getting closer. She hears the cow's loud chewing. Nanny peeks up and sees a cow for the first time!

Nanny runs and runs across the grassy field to get away from the big animal, but then she sees other animals just like it all through the field. Nanny hops over a fence at the other side of the field. When she stops running, Nanny is far away from the cows. But she is also far away from Billy and the other goats.

Nanny tries to find something she can climb. She looks around for a good lookout spot, someplace high where she can see the whole farm. But this field is flat and open.

Goat Kids

Farm Stories

Goat Kids

Nanny wanders through the field toward the barn. She sees a cluster of puffy, white animals in the distance. As she gets closer to them, Nanny sees her mother standing among the sheep.

Nanny leaps to her mother's side. Mama Goat stands over a newborn lamb. The woolly, round sheep peer at Nanny, but she is safe now.

At the end of the day the farmer is surprised to see Nanny with her mother. The farmer pats Nanny on the head and leads Nanny and her mother back toward the brushy field.

In the field, Billy is as full as he can be. Billy was so busy chewing the tasty brush, he did not notice that Nanny had left the field. The goats have done a good job of clearing the tough brush from the field. The farmer leads all the goats back toward the barn.

Farm Stories

Back inside the barn Nanny settles down in the bed of hay. She is glad to be back at the barn. Nanny is tired from her busy day of jumping and exploring new places on the farm.

Billy is so full from his busy day in the field that he cannot eat another thing. He does not even want to go to his favorite places, the bins filled with hay and grain. Instead, he sits near Nanny in the soft hay. Soon their mother joins them there.

It has been a busy day for all of them. Mama Goat has helped the newborn baby lamb. Billy has worked with the other goats to help the farmer clear the field of tough bushes and weeds. And Nanny has met the big cows and fluffy sheep for the very first time!

Mama Goat and her two goat kids curl up in the hay, where they sleep soundly all night long.

Goat Kids

The next morning the farmer arrives early for the milking. When he is finished he walks over to pat Nanny and Billy.

"Your mother will be busy with the baby lamb again today," he tells them. "I am sure you two kids will find a way to keep busy, too. Just stay out of trouble."

The farmer leads their mother out to the pasture. Billy and Nanny run out to the barnyard.

What will Billy and Nanny do today? After a long rest Billy is hungry again. Nanny wants to jump and climb again. But today they want to stay together.

On the other side of the barn Nanny and Billy carefully climb up large wooden blocks stacked next to a tree. From there Nanny can see everything and Billy can munch on the tree's tender leaves. Now they can do what they like best—together!

Goat Kids

Mary, Mary, Quite Contrary

Ma- ry, Ma- ry, quite con- tra- ry, how does your gar-den

grow? With sil- ver bells and coc- kle shells, and

pret-ty maids all in a row.

Mary, Mary, Quite Contrary

Pussycat, Pussycat

Pus-sy-cat, pus-sy-cat, where have you been? I've been to Lon-don to

vis- it the Queen. Pus-sy-cat, pus-sy-cat, what did you there? I

fright-ened a lit- tle mouse un- der her chair.

Farm Kitten

Illustrated by Debbie Pinkney
Written by Catherine McCafferty
and Brian Conway

Farm Stories

Today is a special day! In a warm, quiet corner of the barn Mama Cat nestles in the hay and gives birth to five kittens. Mama Cat dries Farm Kitten and his sisters' wet fur with her tongue.

Even though their eyes are not open the kittens use their sense of smell to find their favorite spot to be. They cuddle up to Mama Cat's belly. Each kitten picks its place to nurse. Nursing is important since Mama Cat's milk keeps the kittens from getting sick.

When the kittens get older Mama Cat will teach them how to become mousers and help the farmer. Mousers catch mice and rats that eat the farmer's corn and grains.

For now the five new farm kittens are happy to sleep and eat beside their mother in the barn.

Farm Kitten

Farm Kitten

Farm Kitten is two weeks old now. His eyes are open and he can hear. But Farm Kitten still stays close to Mama Cat. He mews to his sisters, and they sleep together in a pile of warmth and comfort.

Mama Cat needs to find food for herself so her milk will be fresh and healthy for her growing kittens. While she goes out to the field to catch a mouse or a rat, Mama Cat leaves her kittens safe in the barn.

There they sleep and keep each other company for a short time. The kittens are still too young to follow their mother on her hunting trip.

Mama Cat has caught a rat today. She carries it back to the barn and shows her kittens how she caught it. Farm Kitten watches his mother carefully. He also learns how the rat moves. All of the kittens will need to hunt for themselves someday.

Farm Stories

Farm Kitten is now four weeks old and ready to explore. He steps out of his soft bed of hay. There are so many new sounds and sights and smells!

Farm Kitten hears a noise in one of the stalls. He jumps up on the stall divider and swings his tail sideways to keep his balance. In the stall he sees a huge brown cow! What a big animal!

Farm Kitten curves his back so he can look big and scary. He fluffs up the hair on his back and tail. But the big brown cow does not run away.

Farm Kitten shows his tiny teeth and hisses as loudly as he can. The big cow just keeps chewing her hay. She is not afraid of Farm Kitten.

Farm Kitten looks down from his high place. He stretches as far as he can toward the ground, then slides the rest of the way down the stall.

Farm Kitten

Farm Kitten

Out in the barnyard Farm Kitten smells the muddy wallow that the pigs are enjoying. As Farm Kitten tries to get a closer look, one of those sloppy pigs trots past him. Splish! Splat! Farm Kitten is covered in soggy, smelly mud!

Farm Kitten finds a dry, quiet spot to wash himself. He wants to clean all the mud from his fur. He also wants to remove the scent the pigs left in the mud.

Smells are very important to cats, and Farm Kitten does not want his sisters or his mother to mistake him for a pig!

Washing also helps to calm Farm Kitten. Cats feel better when their fur is clean. He licks his paw and then wipes his face with it. Farm Kitten tugs at the fur between the pads of his feet to get the mud out. A clean coat will keep Farm Kitten warm and dry.

Farm Stories

When Farm Kitten is finished grooming he sees his mother down by the pond with the rest of the kittens. At last Farm Kitten can watch her hunt. But this is a different kind of hunting. Farm Kitten creeps up to the edge of the pond. He pricks up his ears and watches his mother closely.

Mama Cat looks down in the water for a long time. Suddenly, she darts her paw under the water and throws a flipping, flopping fish up on the grass!

Farm Kitten has never seen a fish before. It splashes him when it moves. Farm Kitten does not like getting wet any more than he likes getting muddy.

But he tries to hunt anyway. Like his mother, he waits to see the fish swim closer. Then he dips his paw in the water. A wet, wiggly fish is not easy to hold onto! All of the fish dart away from Farm Kitten.

Farm Kitten

Farm Kitten

Mama Cat does not want Farm Kitten to be so close to the water. She picks him up by the scruff of his neck and carries him away from the pond. Kittens have loose skin around their necks so Mama Cat can carry them without hurting them.

Farm Kitten's sisters rush over to him once their mother sets him down. It is playtime! Farm Kitten finds a dragonfly. He and his sisters chase the swift flying insect. They leap and swat at its fluttering wings. This game is very good exercise for a kitten that is still learning to hunt.

The other kittens wrestle with one another, trying to hold on with their front paws while they kick with their back paws. Kicking with their back paws helps protect their soft stomachs. Their mother taught them this when they were very young.

Farm Stories

Next the kittens practice creeping up on each other. Stalking in the grass, they crouch down low and wait for just the right moment to pounce.

Farm Kitten tries to move quietly as he sneaks up on his sisters. Lurking and leaping through the field, he pounces again and again. Sometimes he catches one of his sisters. But sometimes he misses!

Suddenly, Farm Kitten spots a big, black bird pecking in the grass. Farm Kitten stays low in the grass, inching closer to the big crow.

Almost ready to pounce, Farm Kitten waves his tail in the air. His swishing tail gives him away. The crow's sharp eyes see the moving tail as a warning. Farm Kitten tries to pounce, but he is too late. The big bird flies away, and all Farm Kitten catches is a pawful of air!

Farm Kitten

Farm Kitten's wagging tail has attracted one of the farm puppies. Even though Farm Kitten and the puppy are both baby animals, they have different body signals.

The puppy does not know that Farm Kitten wags his tail when he is angry. Puppies wag their tails when they are happy and feeling playful.

The puppy gets closer to Farm Kitten, who raises his paw to swat the puppy away. The puppy lifts her paw, wanting to join Farm Kitten in a game. Then the puppy barks to let Farm Kitten know it is playtime.

Farm Kitten does not know the puppy wants to play. He uses his sharp claws to climb up a nearby tree. The puppy can lift her front paws up to the trunk of the tree, but she cannot climb. Farm Kitten waits there for the puppy to go away.

Farm Stories

It has been a busy day, and Farm Kitten is ready for a midday nap. He uses his senses of sight and smell together to help him find his way back to his home inside the barn.

As he gets closer to the barn, Farm Kitten hears a squeak and a rustling of hay. He pricks up his ears and walks slowly into the barn.

It is dark inside, but Farm Kitten can see just fine. Cats have special eyes that help them see at night and in places with dim light.

Just then, Farm Kitten spots a rat at the end of the barn! He creeps closer, using his whiskers to tell him when he is getting too close to objects in the barn. Farm Kitten does not want to bump into things. Any noise could scare away the rat before Farm Kitten has his chance to pounce.

Farm Kitten

Farm Stories

There inside the barn Farm Kitten has another real chance to practice his hunting skills.

He creeps toward the rat at the end of the barn. He is careful not to make too much noise. He stays close to the dark walls and low to the ground, as his mother taught him. Farm Kitten stalks across the dusty barn floor, just like he practiced in the field with his sisters.

When he is close enough to the rat, and ready to pounce, Farm Kitten remembers not to move his tail. Any movement or noise could scare the rat away!

Farm Kitten leaps at the rat. His paw touches the rat's long tail, but the rat wiggles away and runs between the haystacks! The tiny rat can scurry into places that Farm Kitten cannot reach. Now the rat waits for Farm Kitten to go away.

Farm Kitten

Maybe Farm Kitten will catch a rat tomorrow. Now he is too sleepy to wait.

Farm Kitten crawls back to his soft bed of warm hay. There he gently falls asleep. Farm Kitten dreams of his next chance to hunt. He dreams of becoming a true mouser one day.

Farmer in the Dell

The far-mer in the dell, the

far- mer in the dell, hi- ho, the der- ry- o, the

far- mer in the dell.

Farmer in the Dell

Eensy Weensy Spider

The een-sy ween-sy spi- der went
up the wa- ter spout. Down came the rain and
washed the spi- der out. Out came the sun and
dried up all the rain. Now the een- sy ween-sy spi- der went
up the spout a- gain.

Little Honeybee

Illustrated by Andrea Tachiera
Written by Jennifer Boudart
and Brian Conway

The farmer's beehives sit in a field of tall, yellow sunflowers. The beehives do not look very fancy. They are made from stacks of wooden boxes.

Each wooden box has a special bottom, like a screen, which makes it the perfect place for bees to build their home. The bees come and go through an opening at the bottom of the hive.

This hive is home to thousands of honeybees. They live together in a colony.

The honeybees make honey and beeswax that the farmer sells. They feed on the flowers, trees, and vegetable fields on the farm.

By feeding on the plants and carrying the plants' pollen from one flower to another, the honeybees help the plants to grow.

Little Honeybee

Little Honeybee

Honeybees start their lives as tiny eggs. In the spring the young bees begin to hatch. A honeybee does not have eyes, wings, or legs until it is at least two weeks old. At this stage the honeybee looks more like a worm than a bee. Until its eyes, wings, and legs form, the honeybee is called a larva.

The baby bee larva lives in a tiny, six-sided cell made from beeswax. Hundreds of these cells put together make honeycombs. Since the larva cannot leave its cell, the other bees in the hive must come to feed the baby bees that live there.

When the baby bee is almost three weeks old, she crawls out of her cell for the first time. To get out she must eat a small hole through the beeswax that covers one wall of her cell. This is her first job as a honeybee, and it is very hard work for a baby bee!

Farm Stories

The newborn honeybee goes to work right away. She is born knowing what her job is in the hive. The little bee crawls in and out of empty cells. She makes sure each cell is clean. She picks out any dirt that has fallen into the open cells. Each cell needs to be clean before it is filled with honey, and the queen bee will only lay eggs in clean cells.

Young female bees like this bee and her sisters are called workers. They help take care of the hive and gather food. The queen bee is the only bee that lays eggs for the hive. And male bees help the queen to lay her eggs.

The little bee will not leave the hive for three weeks. During this time she is a "house bee." She helps clean the hive. She feeds baby bees. And she builds new cells in the hive with beeswax.

Little Honeybee

Little Honeybee

Beeswax is like cement. The little bee makes the beeswax with her body. She carefully takes bits of beeswax from her belly and builds new cells. Some cells will hold baby bees. Others will store honey and food for the colony.

Once the bees have made more than enough honey to feed themselves and their young, the farmer will take some of the honey away from the hive. He always leaves enough behind for the bees in the colony to eat.

The young honeybee is growing. She is almost ready to leave the hive. She has one last job as a house bee, though. It is a very important job. She must guard the entrance to the hive. Other animals, even other bees, will try to steal honey from the hive.

Farm Stories

As she stands guard, a robber bee from another hive tries to sneak past the little bee to steal food. The little bee touches the robber bee, and right away she knows the bee is not from her colony. The little bee pushes the robber bee away from the hive, and the stranger flies away. The hive is safe again!

The little honeybee is now ready to take her first flight! She is now called a field bee. She will begin to collect food for the hive. When her wings move up and down very fast, they make a buzzing sound. Soon the little bee rises into the air. She circles around the hive many times to learn what her hive looks like so she can find her way back to it. Her next flight will be to the farmer's fields to find food.

Little Honeybee

Little Honeybee

The little honeybee buzzes through the summer air. She is looking for just the right flowers. She looks for flowers with bright colors and a sweet scent. Her special eyes help her find the flowers that are filled with the nectar she needs.

When the little bee finds a clover, she can tell it holds the nectar she needs. She lands and sips the liquid nectar from its flower. Her tongue, shaped like a tube, makes the nectar easy for her to sip.

The little honeybee will fill her tummy with the sweet nectar and then take it back to the hive. The nectar mixes with a special fluid that bees have in their honey stomachs.

The mixture of this fluid and the nectar makes honey. The bees store their honey back in the hive, sealed inside the beeswax cells they have built.

Farm Stories

While the little honeybee collects nectar, she also has another job to do. She gathers pollen and carries it from flower to flower.

The pollen on a flower looks like yellow dust. The pollen sticks to the bee's furry legs. She brushes the pollen back with her front legs. The pollen gathers in little baskets on her back legs.

The bee visits many different flowers when she feeds. Some of the pollen that she has collected from one flower falls onto a new flower. When the pollen from one flower mixes with another, a seed will form. The seed makes a new plant. This is called pollination.

When the little bee's baskets are full she takes her pollen back to the hive. There the pollen will be stored for food.

Little Honeybee

Little Honeybee

The little bee takes the goodies she has found and returns them to the hive. She gives her load of nectar and pollen to a house bee. The house bees carry the foods to honeycomb cells, where they are stored.

The little bee flies farther into the hive so she can tell her brothers and sisters where she found the tasty food. There she does a special dance for them. The dance is one way a honeybee can give the other bees an important message.

The little bee turns in a circle and wiggles her body. The way she moves lets the other bees know how far away they must fly to reach the flowers she found. Her movements also tell the other bees what direction to fly to find the food.

The little bee also gives off a smell that tells the other workers what kind of flowers she found.

It is time for the farmer to collect, or harvest, the honey from the hive. The farmer sprays smoke in the top box of the hive. The little bee does not like the smoke, so she crawls to the bottom of the hive with the other bees.

The smoke also helps to protect the farmer. The smoke makes the bees move very slowly. The farmer is less likely to be stung after he sprays the smoke. The farmer also wears a suit that covers his skin.

The farmer lifts some honey-filled cells from the top box and removes the honey. He leaves behind any cells that hold the queen's eggs and the young honeybees. He also leaves plenty of honey and pollen for the colony to eat.

The farmer takes the honey home, where it will be stored in a jar and sold to customers.

Little Honeybee

After the farmer has harvested as much as he needs, the bees know the hive needs to make more honey. A cloud of worker bees buzzes around the hive. They are getting ready to look for more food.

The little honeybee is with them. This is what she was born to do. She will spend the rest of her life flying in search of food for her big family.

Baby Bluebird

Illustrated by Lisa Harkrader
Written by Cristina Ong

Baby Bluebird looked up at the sky. She watched all the other birds flying. "It is spring," she said. "I should be flying, too, but I do not know how to start."

Her friend Rabbit watched the birds, too. "Flying looks a lot like hopping," said Rabbit. "I see birds hopping about all the time. Practice hopping with me. If you hop high enough, you might start to fly."

Rabbit hopped off through the garden. Then Baby Bluebird hopped after her. She was in the air, but she soon came back down to the ground. Baby Bluebird tried again and again.

"What do you think, Baby Bluebird?" asked Rabbit. "Is hopping like flying?"

"It's a little like flying," said Baby Bluebird. "But I keep landing. I don't think real flying is so bouncy."

Baby Bluebird watched the other birds as they hopped and lifted off the ground. Her friend Gopher watched the birds, too.

"It seems to me," said Gopher, "that flying is a lot like digging. Maybe if you practice digging with me, it will help you learn to flap your wings and fly. And digging is so much fun!"

Baby Bluebird

Gopher popped down into his hole and began to dig through the pasture. "It doesn't look like much fun to me," said Baby Bluebird, "but I'll give it a try."

Baby Bluebird found a nice big patch of dirt. She flapped her wings, trying to dig a hole. But the dirt was too hard, and her feathers were too soft.

All her flapping did not help Baby Bluebird fly, but she did raise a huge cloud of dust in the air. Baby Bluebird coughed and sneezed and wheezed.

"Maybe digging isn't like flying after all," she said.

Baby Bluebird sat down in the grass and looked at the birds taking off. The birds hopped off the ground, then quickly flapped their wings. They flew as if the breezes gently carried them through the air.

"What is their secret?" Baby Bluebird wondered. "I can hop. I can flap my wings. But I still can't fly."

Her friend Turtle watched the birds, too. "Flying looks a little like swimming," he said. "Maybe if you practice swimming through the water with me, it will help you learn to glide through the air when you fly."

Baby Bluebird watched Turtle glide around the pond. "That doesn't look very hard," she said. She jumped in the water. "Oh, my! It's so wet!" she cried.

Baby Bluebird

"Paddle out here to the middle," said Turtle.

Baby Bluebird tried to paddle. She splashed and sputtered and glugged. Baby Bluebird wanted to glide like Turtle. But she couldn't.

"Maybe swimming isn't like flying after all," she said. "I don't think flying is so soggy."

Baby Bluebird pulled herself onto the grassy edge of the pond. She fluttered her wings to dry them.

When her wings were dry, Baby Bluebird went to the farmhouse and found Cat and Dog curled up on the porch. Baby Bluebird sat down beside them and watched the birds flying above her.

The birds playfully swooped through the sky. As they flew, they even sang a pretty song.

"These birds can fly *and* sing," said Baby Bluebird. Cat and Dog watched and heard the birds, too.

"They look happy," said Cat.

"We sing when we're happy," said Dog.

"Maybe singing is part of flying," said Cat. "If you sing loud enough and long enough, maybe you'll begin to fly, too. We'll help you."

Dog howled. Cat yowled. Baby Bluebird tweeted. She took a deep breath and let out a squawk! But nobody started to fly.

"It's no use," said Baby Bluebird. "Singing won't make me fly. I might as well stop trying."

"Thank goodness," said Dog. "I don't have any howls left."

"Stop trying?" said Cat. "You can't stop trying. If you want to fly, you must find a way."

Baby Bluebird sat down on the porch steps and put her head in her wings. But then she looked up.

"Singing wasn't enough. And neither was hopping or flapping or gliding," she said. "But I think I know what I need to do."

Baby Bluebird decided to put together everything she had learned from the other animals. She took a running start. She hopped like Rabbit. She flapped her wings like Gopher.

Suddenly, Baby Bluebird was flying through the air! She glided through the beautiful sky like the other birds she had seen and like Turtle had glided through the water.

"I'm flying!" she chirped. "I never thought I'd be able to do it!"

Baby Bluebird swooped through the clouds. She flitted from tree to tree. Then Baby Bluebird soared above her friends.

Baby Bluebird

"Look at me!" Baby Bluebird called out to Rabbit and Gopher and Turtle. "I finally did it! I can fly!" she chirped to Cat and Dog.

Then Baby Bluebird raised her head and, like Cat and Dog, began to sing. It was the happiest song the animals ever heard.

Little Bo-Peep

Lit-tle Bo-Peep has lost her sheep and does- n't know where to

find them. Leave them a- lone, and they'll come home,

bring-ing their tails be- hind them.

The Cat and the Fiddle

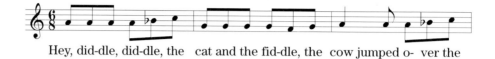

Hey, did-dle, did-dle, the cat and the fid-dle, the cow jumped o- ver the

moon. The lit- tle dog laughed to see such sport, and the

dish ran a- way with the spoon.

Counting Sheep

Illustrated by Kathy Wilburn
Written by Catherine McCafferty

Fleecy was a young lamb who was full of energy. She romped through the meadows every day. And she could run and play all day long.

The crickets and butterflies let her chase them through the fields. None of the other sheep could keep up with the little insects. But pouncing, prancing Fleecy surely could. She never wore out.

At the end of the day Fleecy's friends would fly away. Fleecy wished she could fly like the crickets and butterflies.

She looked at the sky as a wonderful, magical place. Fleecy spent each night staring at it.

Fleecy really thought that someday she might take to the sky and fly. She had so much energy that she stayed awake even when it was time to sleep.

Counting Sheep

Fleecy's mother began to worry about her. "It's not good for a little lamb to stay up so late," her mother told her one night. "A growing lamb needs her sleep."

Fleecy's mother had an idea. She knew that Fleecy had a fondness for the sky. "Look up to the sky," she said, "and count the stars you see. I'm sure you'll fall asleep soon."

Counting Sheep

Fleecy gazed at the bright stars in the night sky. She imagined that she sailed from star to brilliant star, tapping each one as she counted it.

"One, two, three," Fleecy counted. She only got to three before she slipped off to sleep.

Fleecy's mother was right. Fleecy slept so well that she had more energy than ever the next day.

"I flew higher than a butterfly in my dream last night," she told her friends.

That night when it was time for sleep, there were no stars to count. Fleecy was very disappointed. She hoped to fly in her dreams and touch more stars.

Again, Fleecy could not sleep. Even after a busy day with the butterflies, Fleecy was still full of energy.

Counting Sheep

Fleecy's mother noticed how restless the little lamb was. "Try counting the clouds tonight," said Fleecy's mother. "That should help you get to sleep."

Fleecy watched the clouds slowly crossing the night sky. She imagined she was with them, soaring high above the field. In her thoughts she jumped and flew from cloud to cloud. To Fleecy every cloud was a soft, cool pillow puff that wrapped gently around her.

She leaped from one cloud pillow to another. She even leaped over the moon. "I thought only cows did that," Fleecy giggled. And then she remembered what her mother told her. She could not just play in the clouds. She had to count them if she wanted to fall asleep.

"One, two, three," she counted as she hopped among the clouds. Fleecy only got to three before she was fast asleep.

Sure enough, Fleecy's mother was right again! Counting the clouds really did help Fleecy fall asleep. Once again Fleecy slept soundly all through the night. She woke up cheerful and full of energy, ready for another busy day.

"Last night I couldn't fly among the stars," Fleecy told her friends in the meadow. "So I hopped from cloud to cloud instead. Tonight I'm going to fly to the clouds at the tippety-top of the sky!"

But the next night there were no clouds. There weren't any stars, either.

"How will I get to sleep now?" Fleecy asked her mother. "There's nothing in the sky for me to count."

Counting Sheep

Fleecy's mother thought for a moment, then she said, "Why don't you try counting the sheep? We'll always be here, even when the stars and the clouds are gone."

Fleecy lay down in the grassy meadow. Her mother was right. The sheep were always there. But they did not seem like a very fun thing to count.

Sheep were not bright and sparkly like the stars way up in the sky. They did not float and soar above her like the clouds.

"But sheep are puffy like clouds," Fleecy thought. "And soft."

Fleecy snuggled in close to her mother. "Maybe I'll try counting them just this once," Fleecy said.

Counting Sheep

Fleecy started counting all the sheep sleeping in the grass around her. She imagined that she floated high above the field, and the sleeping sheep rose up with her as she counted them.

In her thoughts, every sheep's white woolly coat was a puffy cloud on the dark night sky. The floating sheep winked at her, and their bright eyes sparkled like the stars.

"One, two, three," Fleecy counted as she floated with the other sheep.

Fleecy only got to three before she was sleeping soundly, just like the rest of the sheep.

From then on, Fleecy's mother never had to worry about Fleecy being restless. And she never again heard Fleecy complain when there were no stars or clouds in the sky.

That's because Fleecy counted sheep every night. She snuggled close to her mother in the grass and imagined she was a woolly cloud that was rising high up in the sky.

Fleecy imagined the other sheep were woolly clouds, too, and Fleecy counted them as they rose from the field to join her.

"One, two, three," she counted as she dozed off.

Each night Fleecy only got to three before she was fast asleep. She always slept well, dreaming that she was floating restfully among the soft, puffy clouds with the winking, twinkling eyes.

She soared high in the sky and danced among the stars. Sometimes she even leaped over the moon.

And Fleecy always had plenty of energy in the daytime, too.

"I floated to the tippety-top of the sky last night," she told the insects while she chased them. "And someday I'll fly just like you!"

Though she tried again and again, Fleecy was never able to fly like her friends in the meadow did. But in her starry dreams she came closer to flying than any little lamb ever had.

Farm Stories

Baa, Baa, Black Sheep

Baa, baa, black sheep, have you any wool? Yes, sir, yes, sir, three bags full. One for the mas-ter, and one for the dame, and one for the lit-tle boy who lives down the lane.

Baa, Baa, Black Sheep

Be Kind to Your Web-Footed Friends

Be kind to your web-footed friends, for a duck may be some-body's mo-ther. Be kind to the ducks in the swamp, where the weather's dark and damp. You may think this is the end... well, it is!

Tiny Gosling

Illustrated by Anastasia Mitchell
Written by Jennifer Boudart
and Brian Conway

Two geese guard a nest of eggs. One of the geese is bigger than the other. He is the gander, or male goose. The gander guards the smaller goose. She is his mate for life.

Mother Goose sits down on her nest while the gander stands guard. The gander is the father of the baby geese that are growing inside the eggs. They are almost ready to hatch. Father Gander protects his mate and their precious eggs.

Mother Goose has kept the eggs warm for almost one month, turning them each day. This helps the baby geese, or goslings, grow properly in their eggs. Today Mother Goose feels her eggs bumping and turning in the nest beneath her. It is time for her eggs to hatch!

Tiny Gosling

Tiny Gosling

The first egg rattles and shakes. Then a tiny crack opens on the side. Tiny Gosling's little orange beak pokes through the egg. Next, he pushes his tiny head through the shell. Tiny Gosling must break out of the hard shell without any help from Mother Goose or Father Gander.

Finally, Tiny Gosling wiggles his whole body out of the cracking shell, and the egg breaks open. Tiny Gosling's feathers are very wet. He blinks his little eyes. Then he lies on his side to rest.

Tiny Gosling is very tired. Cracking the egg is hard work for a newborn gosling like him.

Tiny Gosling's brothers and sisters are breaking free of their eggs, too. One by one the little goslings push their way out of their shells. All ten eggs hatch in one day.

Farm Stories

Tiny Gosling and the others are dry in a few hours. Their feathers are soft and fuzzy. The nest is full now, with ten wiggling little goslings!

Mother Goose has lined the nest with small, soft feathers from her own body. The small feathers that she uses to make their bed are called down. During the first hours of life Mother Goose covers her new family with her body. The goslings are warm and safe beneath her wings.

If Mother Goose has to leave the nest, she covers her goslings with straw and feathers. They keep her babies warm and well-hidden.

Father Gander keeps the other animals away from the nest. If any animals get too close, Father Gander flaps his wings and honks loudly. It is a signal for the other animals to stay away!

Tiny Gosling

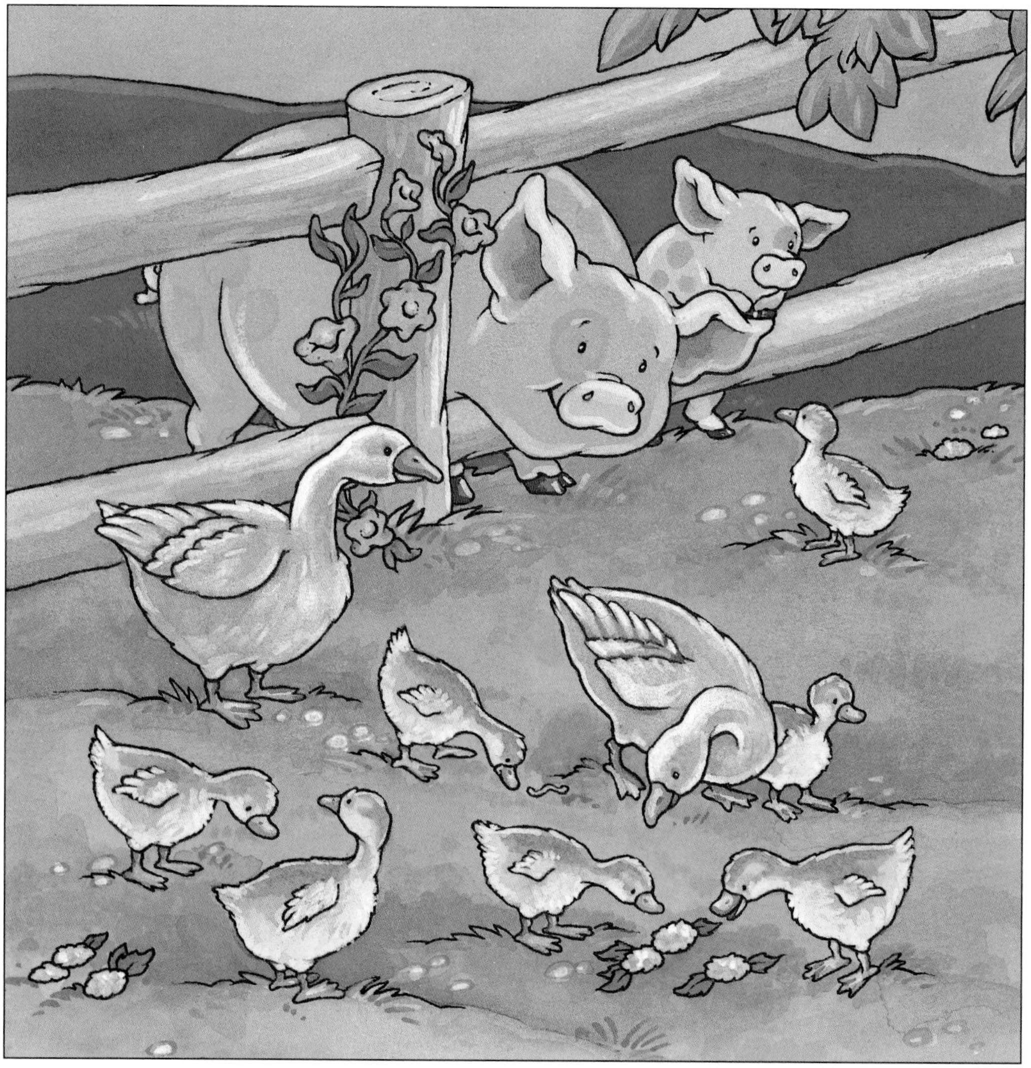

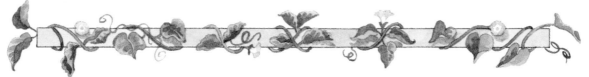

Tiny Gosling

Now that Tiny Gosling and his brothers and sisters are warm and dry, they wiggle their way out of their nest. They are hungry and want to find food!

Goslings can feed themselves from the time they are born. Mother Goose knows what her goslings need. She leads them into the barnyard. She shows them the best way to pull at the grass and weeds.

Sometimes the farmer lets the geese snack on the weeds on his farm. They help to keep his barnyard clean. The geese gladly do that job for the farmer.

The edges of a goose's bill are shaped like a saw. That makes it much easier to tear plants. While Tiny Gosling eats he swallows bits of stone and dirt with his food. These bits do not hurt Tiny Gosling. They help to grind the food into smaller pieces. Then the geese can digest their food more easily.

Farm Stories

In the morning Mother Goose takes the goslings to the pond. Goslings can swim when they are only one day old. Tiny Gosling is the first one to go into the pond. He dips his head under first. Then he dips his whole body under the water. Tiny Gosling shakes his fuzzy feathers as the cool pond water trickles across his back.

Tiny Gosling is ready to move into deeper water. He begins paddling with his tiny, webbed feet. Tiny Gosling is swimming for the first time!

Soon all his brothers and sisters join him in the pond. They hop from the shore and drop into the water. They paddle to catch up with their brother.

As the goslings swim together, they take small sips of water with their beaks and lift their heads so the water can slide down their long necks.

Tiny Gosling

Farm Stories

Tiny Gosling

Now Tiny Gosling is almost eight weeks old. He has grown new feathers in place of the short, fuzzy ones. Tiny Gosling looks more like his parents now, but he will not be full-grown until he is almost two years old!

Tiny Gosling will be able to fly soon. But he will never fly away from the farm where he was born. The farm will always be his home.

Sometimes the geese protect their home. They act as watchdogs for the farmer!

One day Tiny Gosling sees a strange animal. It is a cat that is looking for food. When the stranger comes closer Tiny Gosling springs into action. He runs at the cat with his neck stretched out and his wings flapping. He honks and hisses as loud as he can. The cat runs away!

When the big cat has gone away, Tiny Gosling starts to relax. He settles down and begins to rub his beak over his feathers. He starts near the base of his tail and collects a special oil onto his beak. Then he spreads the oil all over his feathers. This is called preening.

Tiny Gosling does this again and again. He takes his time so he will not miss any spots. This oil keeps his feathers waterproof.

Tiny Gosling takes good care of his feathers to keep them clean and neat. He pulls out any dead feathers and picks off tiny bugs.

Tiny Gosling likes to clean his feathers. It makes him feel better. It also helps to keep him healthy. If his feathers are in good shape they will keep him warm in the winter.

Tiny Gosling

Tiny Gosling

Tiny Gosling meets his brothers and sisters in the barnyard. He watches them settle down with the other geese for an afternoon nap. Tiny Gosling is not tired just yet. He wants to explore the farm.

When he sees a friendly butterfly flutter through the barnyard fence, Tiny Gosling waddles out of the barnyard to follow it.

Tiny Gosling wanders into the farmer's front yard. There he finds many crunchy weeds popping up from the long, green grass! These weeds look better than the ones in the barnyard. Tiny Gosling is ready for an afternoon snack. He waddles through the grass to the tastiest weeds.

Just then, the farmer's dog comes around the corner of the house. Tiny Gosling does not see the big dog coming toward him at all!

Farm Stories

The farmer's dog is only watching Tiny Gosling. It is the dog's job to watch over the farmer's yard. The dog makes sure the other animals stay where they are supposed to be, in the barnyard or in the fields.

The dog knows that a goose should not be grazing without the farmer's permission. The farmer does not allow any of his animals to graze in his front yard!

The farmer's dog comes up from behind Tiny Gosling and gives him a nudge. Tiny Gosling is very surprised by the big dog! He runs back toward the barnyard, honking and flapping his tiny wings.

The dog trots behind Tiny Gosling, following him back to the barnyard. Once Tiny Gosling reaches the barnyard the farmer's dog runs back to the house.

Tiny Gosling is very tired now. Maybe he should take a nap after all.

Tiny Gosling

When Tiny Gosling is not eating or taking a bath in the cool pond, he is sleeping. As he sleeps, he tucks his head behind his little wing.

One of his tiny round eyes opens lazily from time to time. Tiny Gosling checks to make sure his sisters and brothers are nearby. Life on the farm is good for this young goose.

Little Red Hen

Illustrated by Tammie Speer-Lyon
Written by David Presser
and Lisa Harkrader

Little Red Hen lives happily on a farm along with her three young chicks. They like to help each other whenever there is work to be done around the farm. And when all the work is finished Little Red Hen and her chicks like to sing and play and eat the delicious food they have grown.

On the farm there also lives a dog, a cat, a horse, and a mouse. The animals are all happy together. But when the time comes to do the chores the other animals never seem to lend a hand. Little Red Hen and her chicks do all the work themselves.

On this sunny spring day Little Red Hen gathers some seeds and puts them into a pail. She fetches her rake and her hoe from the barn. Then she sets out for the field to plant the seeds.

When she gets there, Little Red Hen finds the dog sleeping in his doghouse.

"Who will help me plant these seeds?" asks Little Red Hen.

"Not I," says the dog as he yawns and walks out of his doghouse and stretches in the grass.

"Then I will do it myself," says Little Red Hen.

Little Red Hen begins planting the seeds in a neat row. Before long, her three chicks come by.

"We will help you," chirp the chicks. The chicks start to work. They scratch the ground with their feet and peck out holes for the seeds.

By the end of the day they have planted every last seed. They gather the rake and hoe and pail and head back home. After all their hard work Little Red Hen and her chicks enjoy their best night's sleep ever.

Several busy months pass for Little Red Hen and her chicks. They water the seeds they planted and pull any weeds in the field.

Soon Little Red Hen and her chicks can see tiny green shoots sprouting up from the ground. The shoots grow and grow.

Before they know it autumn has arrived on the farm. After months of careful tending, the tiny green shoots have grown into tall, slender stalks of wheat.

Little Red Hen

Little Red Hen and her three chicks take their cart to the field to harvest the wheat. When they get there Little Red Hen and her chicks find the cat in the field. The cat is licking her paws. The dog is nearby in his doghouse, taking an afternoon nap.

Little Red Hen and her chicks roll their cart up to the edge of the field. The field is large, and the wheat stalks are very tall. Little Red Hen is afraid that she and her chicks cannot harvest that much wheat all by themselves.

"Who will help me harvest all this wheat?" asks Little Red Hen.

"Not I," says the cat as she swishes her tail back and forth.

"Not I," says the dog as he scratches behind his ear with his paw.

"Then I will do it myself," says Little Red Hen.

"We will help you!" peep her chicks, and they set off to work.

Little Red Hen and her three little chicks harvest the wheat all by themselves. They cut the wheat stalks one by one. They pull the wheat kernels from the stalks one by one. They pile the kernels into the cart one by one.

The cat sits by and watches. The dog is back in his doghouse, fast asleep.

It is hard work, but Little Red Hen and her chicks do not stop. By the end of the day Little Red Hen and her chicks are very tired. But they have a whole cart full of wheat, so they go home happy.

Little Red Hen

The next day Little Red Hen and her chicks take their cart full of wheat to the mill.

Little Red Hen pulls the cart, while her three little chicks push from behind with all their might. They push and pull, and pull and push, all the way to the mill.

Farm Stories

Slowly but surely, Little Red Hen and her chicks get to the mill. They unload their cart so their wheat can be ground into flour. When it is time to go home there are so many bags of flour that their cart is filled to the top.

Once again, Little Red Hen pulls the cart. And once again, her three little chicks push from behind with all their might. They push and pull, and pull and push, up hills and over streams, until they finally get back home.

At the farm they find the horse standing in the barn. He is munching some oats and swatting flies off of his back with his tail. The cat and the dog are both lying nearby in the hay.

Little Red Hen and her chicks start to push the cart into the barn.

Little Red Hen

"Who will help me unload this flour?" asks Little Red Hen.

"Not I," says the horse as he munches.

"Not I," says the cat.

"Not I," says the dog.

"Then I will do it myself," says Little Red Hen.

"We will help you," chirp the chicks, and they begin to work.

Little Red Hen and her three chicks unload the flour, bag by bag, into the barn. It is hard work for one mother hen and her three little chicks, but it is fun working together. By the end of the day they have unloaded all the bags. They stack them neatly in the corner of the barn.

"Now we will have enough flour to last all winter long," says Little Red Hen.

Little Red Hen

Little Red Hen and her chicks rise early the next morning. They carry one of the bags of flour from the barn to the house.

The horse, the cat, and the dog follow Little Red Hen and the chicks into the kitchen. The horse rests by the door. The cat sits in the windowsill. The dog lies on the rug. They watch Little Red Hen and her chicks make bread.

First Little Red Hen and the three chicks pour some of the flour into a big bowl. Then they add water and eggs and salt and yeast. They mix it all up into bread dough. When Little Red Hen looks in the cupboard for some sugar, she finds the mouse running around inside.

"Who will help me knead the bread?" Little Red Hen asks all the animals.

"Not I," says the mouse as he hops out of the cupboard.

"Not I," says the horse.

"Not I," says the cat.

"Not I," says the dog.

"Then I will do it myself," says Little Red Hen.

"We will help you," peep her chicks, and they begin to work.

Little Red Hen adds the sugar, and the chicks mix it in. They take turns kneading the dough. When the dough is ready Little Red Hen shapes it into a loaf. Then she places the loaf in a pan and puts it into the oven to bake.

Farm Stories

Little Red Hen and her three chicks wash the bowl and clean up the kitchen. Soon the wonderful smell of baking bread drifts through the house and out into the barnyard.

The smell makes all the other animals hungry. The mouse sniffs. The horse whinnies. The cat purrs. And the dog licks his lips.

When the bread is finished baking, Little Red Hen takes it out of the oven and places it on the table. It looks as delicious as it smells!

Little Red Hen and her three chicks gather around the table. "Who will help me eat this bread?" asks Little Red Hen.

"We will!" say the mouse, the horse, the cat, and the dog. They cannot wait to taste the bread. It smells so good!

Little Red Hen

"Anyone who helped me plant the seeds in the field can help me eat the bread," says Little Red Hen.

"We helped!" chirp the chicks. They each slice off a piece of bread and spread it with jam and butter. The mouse, the horse, the cat, and the dog watch as the chicks eat the bread. "Could we have some, too?" they ask.

"Anyone who helped me harvest the wheat can help me eat the bread," says Little Red Hen.

"We helped!" chirp the chicks. They each slice off a piece of bread and spread it with jam and butter. The mouse, the horse, the cat, and the dog watch again as the chicks eat the bread.

"Is it our turn now?" they ask.

"Anyone who helped me unload the flour or bake the bread can help me eat it," says Little Red Hen.

"We helped do both of those things!" chirp the chicks. They each slice off a third piece of bread and spread it with jam and butter. Now there is only one piece left.

The mouse, the horse, the cat, and the dog watch the chicks eat. Their tummies growl. "Who gets to eat the last piece?" they ask.

"I planted, harvested, unloaded, and baked," says Little Red Hen. "I get the last piece." Then she picks up the bread and pops it into her mouth.

Little Red Hen

Little Red Hen sees how sad the other animals look. "We have enough flour for this year," says Little Red Hen. "But next spring we will have to plant more seeds. Who will help me?" she asks.

"We will!" chirp the chicks.

"And we will, too!" say the mouse, the horse, the cat, and the dog.

Three Blind Mice

Three blind mice, Three blind mice.

See how they spin. See how they spin! They

pin the tail on the kit- ty cat, while wear- ing sil- ly par- ty hats. Did you

ev- er see such a sil- ly sight as three blind mice?

The Old Gray Mare

Speedy Colt

Illustrated by Erin Mauterer

Title page illustrated by Lyn Martin

Written by Catherine McCafferty

Speedy was a lively colt. He lived on a farm with many horses. Speedy's whole family lived there, and so did other families with their little colts.

Speedy and his friends were born in the early spring, and they enjoyed their very first summer together. The colts had nothing much to do but play all day in the fields.

Speedy had a best friend named Lightning. Speedy and Lightning were growing bigger and stronger every day.

"Come on, Lightning!" said Speedy. "Let's play chase with the others."

All the colts tore around the fields chasing each other. They loved to play chase together.

Farm Stories

Speedy and Lightning were the fastest little colts on the farm. They raced way ahead of the other colts. Then they circled back to their friends and played chase with them some more.

One day Speedy's mother said, "Speedy, you always seem to enjoy yourself when you play with your friends. I'm glad to see you play with them all day in the sunshine. You have grown into a big, strong colt."

"Thank you, Mother," said Speedy. "My best friend Lightning is as fast as I am!"

Speedy started off to the field where Lightning was waiting for him. But his mother called after him.

Speedy Colt

"Not so fast, Speedy," said his mother. "I have something important to talk to you about."

Speedy came back to his mother. "Sorry, Mother," he said. Speedy waited to hear what she had to say.

"Son," said his mother, "your grandfather would like to spend some time with you and show you around the woods."

"But Mom," said Speedy, "Grandpa is so slow! He doesn't play chase, and he can't race! He's not very much fun."

"Your grandfather may be slow, but that doesn't mean he isn't fun," said Speedy's mother. "And he would really enjoy your company."

"I really love Grandpa," said Speedy. "I want him to be happy. I promise I'll visit with him tomorrow."

"That would be a very nice thing to do, Speedy," said his mother.

Speedy ran off to the path. Lightning and the other colts were waiting for him there.

Speedy Colt

First they played chase together. Then Speedy and Lightning raced each other. Speedy won the first race, and Lightning won the second one.

The next day Speedy forgot about the promise he made to his mother. He and his friends played all day without a care.

Speedy and Lightning raced each other to the edge of the field, where the woods began. Then Speedy remembered that his grandfather wanted to show him the woods. "I will keep my promise tomorrow!" Speedy thought to himself. "Today I'll explore the woods with Lightning."

But Lightning did not want to go into the woods. "Then I'll go on my own," Speedy said as he trotted off down the path.

Speedy whinnied with joy as he trotted further into the woods down the wide path.

But he ran so fast that he was soon very far from where he had been before. Speedy was not sure which way to turn to get back to the field.

First he tried one path, then he tried another. No matter which way he tried, he was still in the woods.

Speedy began to get scared. He tried not to cry. Speedy did not know when he would see his mother and his grandfather again.

Just then Speedy heard the steady clip-clop of a horse walking down the path. It was his grandfather! "Grandpa!" said Speedy. "I was lost, but you found me!"

"Good to see you," said his grandfather. "Lightning told me that he waited for you for a long time. I just thought I'd come and meet you!"

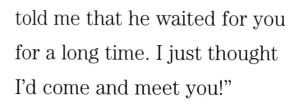

"Why aren't you lost, too?" asked Speedy.

"I know every path on the farm and in these woods," said his grandfather.

"Perhaps I can take you and Lightning on a long walk through the woods tomorrow," he said.

"That's great!" said Speedy. "I guess there's more to life than running around, huh, Grandpa?"

"Sometimes you just need to slow down," said Grandpa, "and spend more time with your family."

Puppy Tale

Illustrated by Kathy Wilburn
Written by Catherine McCafferty

Sparky lived on a farm in the country. He was as curious and as busy as a little puppy could be. Sparky searched and sniffed his way around every inch of that big farm.

One day Sparky's father asked him, "Son, what in the world are you looking for?"

"I smell something that smells like fun," Sparky answered. "I don't know what it is, but I'll know when I find it." And off he went to search.

Sparky's father chuckled. He remembered when he himself was the busiest pup in the litter. At least Sparky was not bothering the cows at milking time or rolling in the mud with the pigs or causing trouble in the henhouse! The busy puppy's silly search kept him out of trouble for a while.

A little later, on the other side of the meadow, Sparky caught a brand new scent.

Sparky did not know what the scent was, but he knew that it smelled like something fun!

Sparky traced the scent into the woods at the edge of the meadow. He dipped his little sniffer into a big pile of dry leaves.

There was something fun in there! Sparky decided to jump right in!

"I know you're in there," he said, sniffing and digging deeper into the pile of old leaves. At last Sparky found his treasure! It was an old toy bone, big and blue and lots of fun!

Puppy Tale

Puppy Tale

Sparky rushed back to the pasture, dragging his new bone all the way. "Look, Dad!" Sparky called. "I found a fun toy!"

"Well, what do you know," Sparky's father said. "I haven't seen that bone in years! That was my toy bone when I was a pup!"

Sparky's father had lost that toy bone long ago. He had searched for it everywhere way back then, but he never caught the slightest scent of it.

"It was buried in the woods beside the meadow," Sparky said. "Like buried treasure!"

"Son, I'm proud of you," said Sparky's father. "You are one fine finder!"

"Can I have it?" Sparky asked.

"You found it, so it's yours," his father said. "Just be sure you take care of it. Don't lose it like I did."

Sparky promised he would never lose his new toy. He kept it with him all the time.

Sparky brought the bone to breakfast. He brought the bone to bed. He held it during nap time, and he carried it while he did his chores. Sparky even brought the bone to the pasture, where he and his family watched the sheep each day.

But Sparky did not watch the sheep. He chomped on the bone most of the time, and when he was not busy chewing, he kept an eye on it. He did not want to lose it. Sparky's brother and sister did not like the bone. Sparky thought they must be jealous.

Puppy Tale

Puppy Tale

Sparky had the bone, and his brother and sister did not. So Sparky offered to share it with them. "We don't want it," they told Sparky. "We want to play circle-chase. But you never play with us anymore!"

Sparky said he would play with them for a little while. Every time he turned, though, Sparky bumped his brother and sister with the big toy bone.

Sparky's father said, "Son, you can't keep running around with that toy bone all the time. I think someone might get hurt by it one of these days."

"But I don't ever want to lose it," said Sparky.

Sparky's father brought him to the edge of the meadow. "We'll dig a hole that you can use to hide your bone," said Sparky's father. "Whenever you want it, all you have to do is dig it up again. This way you don't have to carry it around all the time."

"This is great!" said Sparky. "Now I can leave the bone, and only I will know where it is."

"Don't forget where you buried it, Sparky," his father reminded him.

Puppy Tale

"I promise I won't forget," Sparky said. "I will never lose my favorite toy!"

Sparky barked happily, calling his brother and sister out to the meadow. They came to see what was going on.

"Now I can play with you again!" Sparky called cheerfully. "How about a game of circle-chase?"

"What happened to your toy bone?" his sister wondered.

"You didn't lose it, did you?" asked his brother.

Sparky smiled at his father. "I can't tell you where it is because it's in a secret place, just like a buried treasure. If you ever want to play with it, just let me know. I'll know where to find it!"

Sparky jumped to chase his brother, snapping playfully at his feet.

Sparky's brother chased their sister, and their sister chased Sparky.

And nobody bumped into anyone else! It had been awhile since they had so much fun together.

They played circle-chase all day long. Sparky had been so busy with his new toy bone, he had forgotten what fun it was to play with his family!